ANIMALS HAVE THEIR SAY

KINGA MARTIN ♡

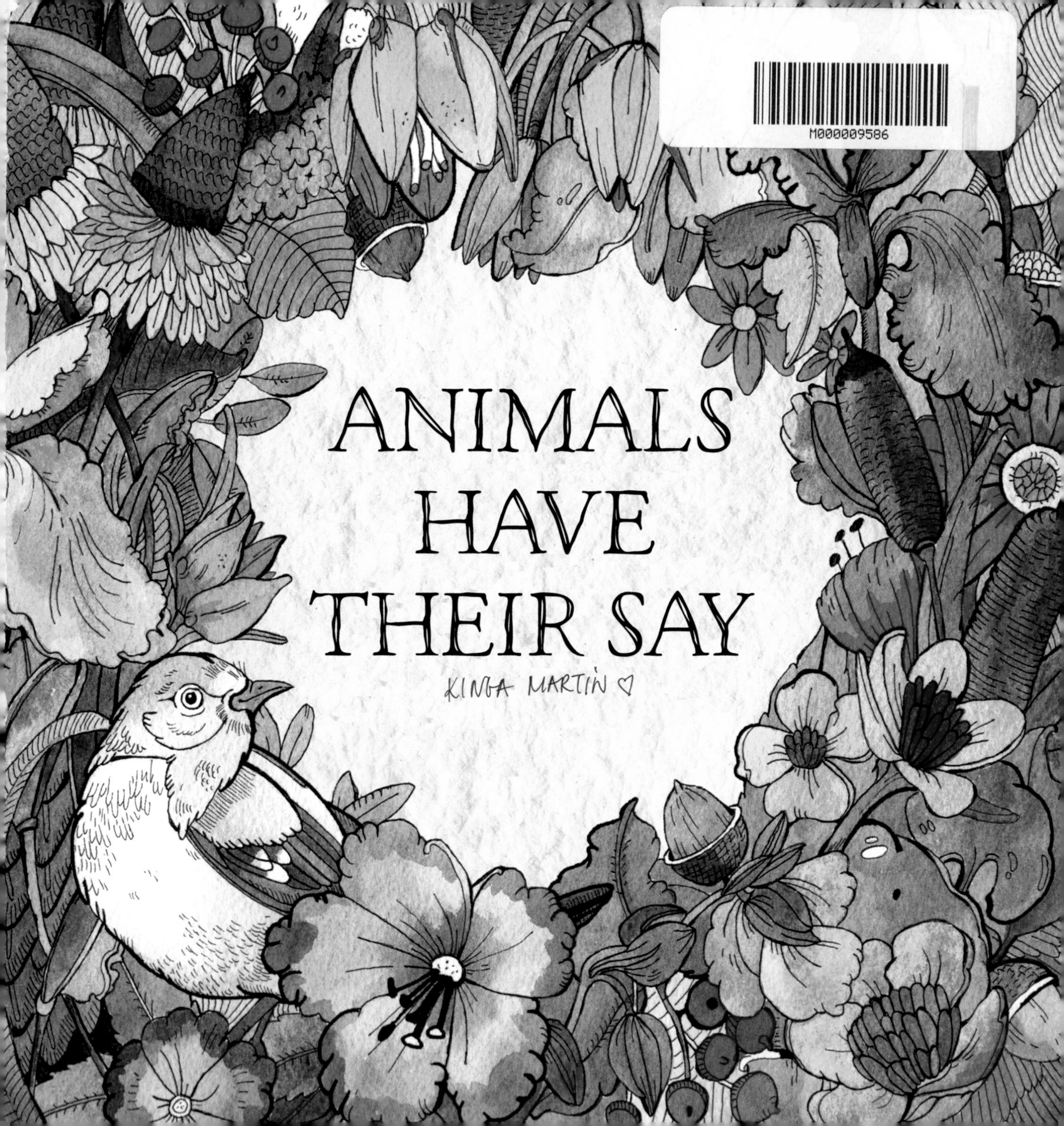

Poems written by Penelope Tanquary Evans
Illustrations by Kinga Martin
Book Design by Kyla Korytoski
Edited by Sara Rauch
Photography by Matthew Duffy Photography

ISBN 1-10951001301
Published by Kingarooart
www.kingarooart.com

ACKNOWLEDGEMENT

I would like to thank first and foremost my friend Jessica Chaloux who has inspired me through her journey fighting cancer to write some of the poems in this book. I would also like to thank Kinga Martin for encouraging me to write. It is through her art that I decided to write again. When I saw her painting of the "blue heron," I began to incorporate the natural world in child-like verses. Kinga and I decided to write a book combining her beautiful pieces with my poetry.

Writing the book involved a lot of graphic art as well. I would like to thank Kyla Korytoski for this as she does great work and was willing to help create the book. Thanks to Sara Rauch who went through every poem with me to make sure each poem was clear and precise and compliments to Matthew Duffy for providing a profile picture included in my biography.

Finally I would like to thank my family and friends for being supportive of my endeavors.

- Penelope

I would like to dedicate this book to Geoffrey and Pam.

- Kinga

The Big Brown Bear and the Squirrel

The big brown bear says, *"It isn't fair,"*
as it waggles its ponderous weight,
"to shoulder such a heavy load."
The squirrel dashes past the bear
slipping through the forest's thorny snare.

The bear sighs,
"I've got my frightful paws, and my furry coat to wear,
but with my stature so mature and stately,
I cannot climb through these brambles
and snares."

The squirrel waltzes by again,
nimble in leg and smug in face,
saying to the old bear,
"You are but a disgrace."

The bear sits, contemplates
at the wonder of its fate.
So complicit becomes the bear, but the solution is worth the wait.
"I will be okay," says the bear. *"I will just sit and stare*
at the briar before me, slowly slipping
each branch, untangling one by one.
Patience will get me out of the snare,"
says the big old bear.

The Eagle and das Igel

The burly hedgehog
in German is known as the igel.

"A creature of luck, I think I am," it says.
It waddles swiftly
from nothing per se,
not looking for any prey.

The eagle impromptu says, *"I am a creature of hope
for those who like to pray.
I swoon and dive with grace,
stamina is my forte
searching for prey."*

*"You, my spiny one, look tempting today,
but, ouch, your needles have me at bay."*

*"Who are you, igel? An imposter,
I say, for I am the true eagle..."*

The hedgehog pounces, sniffs at the eagle:
*"I may be your namesake in a bit of a
very small way..."*

The Cormorant and the Mockingbird

The cormorant with its ghastly glow
appears to threaten the
mockingbird's mire,
dazzling in the muck as if king of the rampant mist.

"Oh, mockingbird, I will silence you tonight
beneath the murky light.
You'll no longer mock me in your fright."

"I will dance about with majestic talons, lifting them in my glee."

"Your voice will only echo the diligent caw of a crow;
You shall be in awe of me."

"King I am of beauteous ugliness.
Do not mock me out of fear;
the fear you have of the command I bring
forth in my own petrifying lair."

"I am the cormorant in all my ethereal being,
in the swampy bog and in its vast fog."

"I bend my long neck silently beneath the shallow water
while you are wanton in your mocks."

"I shall conquer you
with only a slight nod."

"And you will mock the crow:
Caw caw caw...."

The Bunny and the Skunk

"I am the skunk,
a glandular mess
(scientifically speaking).
I stew and create smells
that scare my friends, at best."

"Yet there's a furry little bunny who follows me
across the meadows and shrubs.
It smooshes down my fur with little licks
of love every time I spray.
Attracted to my glandular strife
with many other creatures,
the bunny says, 'You give me a beautifully scented life.'"

"I smell you, my friend," says the bunny so keen.
"You are spreading your love across my little nostrils
so it seems. How long has it been
since we have been friends?
Your smells are akin
to my own as of late,"
asks the bunny as they prance cordially
over the hills and the glades.

"It's not the same," says the bunny.
Its nose wrinkled in vain.

The skunk lamely spews,
"My glands are stuck in some refrain.
I have to be brave.
It is like the loss of gills
for an ocean-bound fish.
My scents have changed.
They are no more."

"Tis so strange,
my glandular range
(scientifically speaking)."

The bunny's nose lifts above its little buck teeth.
"It's okay, my friend.
There is no leaf I haven't turned over yet without a tear.
Times change and time is but a bet.
I will stick by you through and through,
we are an olfactory bonded pair, we two."

The Raccoon and the Fisher Cat

When you see a sassy raccoon
eating its dinner at noon
know there's a fisher cat awaiting its doom.

Creatures that usually frequent the night in their gloom.
By day they are both a bit of a pest
and not a most wanted guest.

Here's how the story goes
as they fight over garbage in a tangled display.

The raccoon and the fisher cat
have been waiting all day,
fighting for food thrown away.
Watch as they both grow extremely morose,
with hunger and greed,
and begin to sway.

Weak,
they become quite meek

when the children across the street
scream at them, to their dismay,
to go away.

The raccoon and the fisher cat lose control
of their fate.
Together,
they are no longer bold.
They weep in a heap
for they are tired and weak.

In the barrel's unlovely shade
tonight they will sleep
as the sun does fade.

Shall they befriend each other
in their miserable ways?

Don't worry for them.
The very next morning
a trout is thrown out,
and they wake to discover
an odious filet.

The Snake and the Salamander

The salamander in its grandeur
dislikes the snake with its impetuous gander
at how many rocks it can mount
without even a foot to grasp
the smoothness.
Angst plagues the salamander's
thoughts and playfulness!

Meanwhile the snake
slithers to another
world as the meandering landscape
plays upon its scales. Quickly, it
propels itself in a slippery demeanor.
The bright sun lighting up its glossy skin.
It agitates the morels
as it progresses past the stately mushrooms
oblivious to any morals
wrapping itself around the bend
of a crooked limb.

In another manner the salamander saunters;
sticking one foot at a time on the slick dirt,
hiding from the snake beneath a stone so cold.
It budges out of the shade one toe at a time.
It is a quiet stepping rhyme
with the making of each footstep
through the rustling leaves,
playing as it believes.

A strange tale:
one walks by playfully
one glides by menacingly.

An understanding creeps into the salamander's thoughts,
liberating its mental bind
on how quickly the snake moves so sublime.

Avoiding a chance meeting of the snake
between the rock and the sun,
lest the snake's fangs meet its own slimy skin,
The salamander decides to run!

Their stripes are the same.
Yet the salamander feels ashamed.
The snake passes the running salamander in unknowing bliss
with a loud, surprising hiss!

The salamander comes to know the snake is smart.
It knows the snake is suddenly aware of its presence.
The salamander realizes the snake has an important role.
Seemingly showing its innocence,
the salamander now believes
the snake has a saintly heart since
it doesn't strike,
swallowing the salamander whole
or tearing the salamander apart.

The Snail and the Leech

The leech swims pleasantly in the marsh,
filled with little creatures like a beach's jetty,
and waits for something that is out of reach.
A parasite of sorts, devouring the blood
of unsuspecting, unhealthy, vile veins of creatures in the mud,
it makes the critters on the shore healthy again.
It sucks the bad blood out from under the skin.
It fantasizes about the richness of the red murk, diseased.
It knows that with the rouge of filth
it will be appeased.

The snail, inauspicious, suffers from melancholia
and is less vicious.
It says, *"You are my friend hitherto, oh leech.*
Do not go lurking into the vastness, so out of reach.
I will entreat you to many vials of my red blood if you wish."
(Believing it has none, as its blood is but blue...)
It turns to sneak back into its humble home.

Scraping the sides of its slimy vestige, the snail looks back.
"I am sad, you see," it says to the leech.
"No one will befriend me, but you, alas,
are my own kindred entity.
Yet, while you have no shell to grasp your suit,
I am stuck in a smelly old
spiral, an old tarnished boot."

"Forgive me for asking," the delusory snail goes on.
"I only wish to court your wily ways"

along the marsh.
"If you may, if you could,
please, please, please it's actually quite tasty.
I'll offer you the vile blood
of my own skin today."

The leech readily concurs.

The Fox and the Spider

The fox trots in its suit fit with bright colors,
an orange and grey array.
It snoops in the pumpkins,
looking for a goody or two.
A spider comes along,
Frightening with its eight long graceful legs.
"Boo!" it shouts.

The spider tells the fox, *"I wear all black all day as would a witch
on a stormy night, flying across the moon
so bright. Mind you, a beautiful sight."*

"But WHY exactly are you dressed in this way!?"
asks the fox.

*"I am ready to frighten young varmints and
children away on All Hallows Eve.
It is the night of follies, including tricks, you might say
and I am dressed for that sort of play!"*
answers the spider.

The fox knows not what to do.
It is true to the colors it wears and
the words it prepares,
not the sly one it may seem to you.

"Supposedly," says the fox, *"I trick all
with my thoughts,
yet I am only dressed to blend in"*

"with the forest, the leaves, and the river bend,
so as not to be seen
by those same young human kin."

"So scare as you might,
I will stay home tonight,
eating goodies in my
lowly den.
With a carved-out pumpkin head,
a wax candle lit within,
avoiding the art of a devious sin."

The Spaniel and the Mole

Says the spaniel to the mole,
"I am going for a stroll,
but after I will chase you
to the end of days,
or until we find your hole."

"I like to play
in the sun's rays
and dance with my webbed toes
down by the river,
where I swim till twilight glows!"

"Oh! Mole! You I shall search for
in the vast meadows afar,
darting along the river's edge
where there is nothing but a silty, sandy, mossy tar."

"Until we pass upon the shore,
when you surface on the soil,
I'll go down the river quite a ways,
to find you once more," the spaniel murmurs.

The mole whispers back, *"But you'll slip through the day's end*
or
until your bare feet tire."

The spaniel answers,
"No, not so, my feet will not tire.
Our toes shall be mixed in the dirt and dew,
to be together at last in the sunset,
to see the finality of mortality
in its cast within the evening's soul.
From the river's edge,
I shall keep following you back to your hole,
as we grow old."

The White Buffalo and the Fawn

The white buffalo in the evening sun sticks out
like birch wood,
timid in the long prairie grasses
behind the great green trees.

Along skips a fawn in its shadow,
disappearing between the red-brown stems.
The fawn is hidden where it now stands
disguised in the tall pasture it plays
swirling about the trees and mama deer,
with snowflakes dotting its flanks and no fears.

The white buffalo,
conspicuous in its color, follows the ghost
of its own mother,
wishing to have a vast snow
to disappear in and to hide while
lavishing in the cold whiteness
so it can be content.
The snow consoling its heart,
a sacred invisible silence.

The white buffalo's obvious stance is
a heavy lure to its foes.
The red-brown fawn mingles lightly and brightly in the night,
her white spots speak
a kindred voice to the great beast
and they both unite at the break
of a radiant dawn.

The Sea Monkey and the Manatee

The sea monkey and the manatee side by side,
one as big as a tree,
one as small as a bee,
both swallowed in the white ocean tide,
shimmering with a blue-green hue.
The tide comes and settles with them along the break wall.

They grin at their luck
to see such a pretty sight.
Both of their faces with wrinkles
and scars,
they are wise
to their surmise
and know that with all its ambience
comes the storm.

Floating out to sea
in tumultuous waves,
on their faces time
catches its essence,
when they survive
the waves crashing upon them.

Once the great winds stop
and the sea is placid again,
with wistful jollity
their eyes capture
a vast golden horizon
upon the massive currents
moving through infinity.

Matthew Duffy Photography

Penelope Evans is a graduate of the University of MA in Amherst currently living in Easthampton, Mass. She has a BA in English. Her interests are hiking, walking her dog; Pumblechook, traveling, and word play. Gertrude Stein, Shel Silverstein, and Dr Seuss are some of her influences. She is an avid lover of nature who grew up going to bird counts and mushroom hunts with her aunt, once a member of the Audubon Society of Virginia.

Kinga Martin is a watercolor artist and children's book illustrator. Martin was born in Poland, and spent many years in Italy before immigrating to the United States. Martin's early exposure to art was something that she couldn't escape. Coming from a talented family, Martin was accustomed to creativity. Her skills were always appreciated by her teachers and even though she did not choose to study art, she was always driven to paint.

Martin opened her studio in 2016, starting with an Etsy store called Kingarooart, offering pets and people portraits at first. She then turned her subjects to the colorful world of nature, where there is no limitation for imaginative minds. Martin depicts many aspects of nature, with her main subjects being birds. Her artwork shows high attention to detail, vibrant, saturated colors and whimsical pen work.

Martin lives in Easthampton Ma, with her husband, where she creates artwork and illustrates books in her Kingarooart studio.